THE DREAMS
THAT SHAPE US
and Other Stories

LOUISE ZEDDA-SAMPSON

The Dreams that Shape Us and Other Stories
Copyright © Louise Zedda-Sampson 2025
www.LZSPress.com.au
Seaford, Australia

Paperback ISBN: 978-0-6451255-4-2
Hardback ISBN: 978-0-6451255-5-9

Front cover artwork: Lynette Orzlowski

Typesetting and cover design: Wildling Design

A catalogue record for this book is available from the National Library of Australia

Dedicated to the Horror Crits writing group for the unwavering support of each member's writing journey, including my own.

Thank you.

CONTENTS

CONTENTS

Close to You

Illuminated by candlelight, I recite the spell.

I'm summoning true love, together, forever.

Flashes of blood-red, sparks of midnight-black.

Smoke swirls, and the smell—

Oh-oh.

"Wrong page," says the demon.

The 504

Rain hammers the window like small fists, fast and angry. Silver ribbons run down the glass, and in the reflection add lines to my already wrinkled face. I know where each of my lines has come from, though, and can spot the shadow imposters. I've certainly had enough time over the years to reflect.

I turn away, restless. I'm keen to get home now. I've been on the bus too long.

A bike bell rings, shrill and sharp. Who would ride tonight? A young chap boards with his bike. He's a regular on the bus too, from the theatre. Reminds me of my Harold, of what I remember. Memory's a shifting thing. I'm not sure if my picture is accurate anymore.

The boy wears a top hat over short hair, a black suit with coattails and a buttonhole carnation. A white handkerchief sits in his pocket. Traces of pigments, orange and unnatural, dapple his skin. His shoes are black and shiny but don't tap as he walks, even though they look like they should. He's dressed for a Broadway musical, like Fred Astaire. He tips his sodden hat, winks and sits down, his bike close by, a rail against the world.

Harold used to like the theatre. Tears prick at my eyes, fresh and full. His last 'I love you' echoes. I told him I didn't have to go, and neither did he, but he wouldn't listen.

He never really listened.

I turn to the window, looking for a fonder memory than

that of goodbyes.

The idling engine thrums, and with a billow of black smoke, we move away from the kerb.

We travel past familiar places, on a familiar route. As we pass the cemetery, I seek out the young girl, the dancer. I see her in my mind's eye, bright as Shirley Temple, dancing with the theatre boy on the bus. But there's no sign of her tonight.

The lights flicker on and off. The bus shudders but keeps moving.

I wave to the baker as we pass his shop. Every day I wave. He never waves back.

But today, he almost raises his hand.

I think of Harold and the theatre, and fonder times.

<hr>

He ties his apron, ready to start before the birds awaken, as bakers often do. Something makes him look, a feeling of sorts, and that's when he sees it. A bus? He shakes his head to clear the cobwebs. The older he gets, the thicker they become.

Bollocks to a bus! Even though they said there was – a ghost bus, at that – there's never been a bus, not in the thirty years he's looked out this window when he's at work. He stretches his aching back, then clutches as a pain erupts in his chest.

He sees it! The 504, numbers black on a fluorescent strip. A woman on the bus waves. He falls to the ground. And when he hears the splash of the ghostly apparition driving through a large puddle, and the whoosh and groan of the door as it finally opens for him, he finally concedes that the stories must be true.

The Forgotten Sea

The clock on the dash says three-o-five p.m. I'm on time; Rob's late. I start work and make some notes. *Red brick, double-fronted, no fence.* I've been to hundreds of places like this: family homes neglected once the children have fled. *Welcoming... wanting?* Why wanting? I cross *wanting...* out. Four long windows face the street, blinds half closed like lazy eyelids. The driveway widens as it meets the road: yawning, open, inviting.

"I'm waiting for Rob," I tell the house, then wonder why, tapping my pen. It's just a house. *Set in a quiet pocket, this family home will offer—*

The knock on the window makes me jump. I press hard on the steering wheel and my neck pops as I whip around. It takes a second or two to work out the blaring noise is my car horn. Rob stands next to the car, laughing. I shoot him a dirty look and a half smile. "Yeah, good one, Rob."

"C'mon then," he says, opening my car door. "Let's go inside. Pretty ordinary, eh?" He doesn't wait for an answer. "How's it going?"

We fall into easy banter about unimportant things. He's older and treats me as a daughter. Or maybe it's more like I treat him as a father.

The sun disappears behind a cloud as we walk up the driveway. A chill wind rises. Autumn leaves scurry around my feet and I rub my arms, failing to suppress a shiver. I don't know when

I stopped, but Rob's already up the steps.

"What are you doing?" Rob says.

I offer a weak smile and return to my notes. *Carport to covered entranceway, where '70s charm awaits.* A black-and-white rectangular doorbell is mounted on the door frame and the solid-oak door has a metal knocker. The memory claws at something deep inside as I climb the three stone steps. My sister peers through amber panels to the left, face pressed hard against the glass. A shadow moves behind the peephole. I blink and it's all gone. No doorbell. No solid oak. No peephole. And no sister.

"It's vacant. We did the photos earlier," Rob says. He tries several keys in the lock. None of them work. He curses under his breath, mumbles something about them maybe being the wrong keys.

"This one!" he says as the lock yields and the door creeps open. The steady tick of a clock is close but also far away, like an echo. Rob's still hunched at the lock as the door gapes wide.

He looks at me and straightens. "Guess we go inside," he says. "Maybe it's not vacant after all." He says this as a joke, but it's not funny. I already want to turn around and leave.

Large and ugly paisley leaves, amber and white, run in parallel lines on walls. A gold eight-pointed star with a round clock in the centre sits high near the ceiling, keeping a time all of its own. I see myself with a beehive hairdo, a miniskirt and white leather knee-high boots.

As if Rob reads my thoughts, he shakes his head.

A sea of lime-green carpet flows in all directions. *Original carpets in impeccable condition.* A giggle rises from my throat as I slip back all those years. My sister and I are rolling in a similar carpet sea, laughing, diving into its luxurious green depths, lost in the churn of imaginary waves. The soft pile enveloping us, supporting us and keeping us warm.

My father, stern at the helm, glares back at us. He tells us to stop, get up, act our age.

"Bloody cold in here." Rob wrinkles his nose. "And musty. Leave the door open for some fresh air." Rob's stride is brisk as he heads towards the back of the house.

I step around the room divider and continue to work. *Classic '70s features. Amber beer-bottle glasswork separates the entranceway from a large, comfortable lounge…* Sun-tinged orange light fittings match the glass. *An older-style home with period features.*

I bend down and stroke the carpet's thick pile. It's old but so very soft. So many memories. Winter days and heaters and woolly socks. Scrabble on the loungeroom floor. And ice-cream! There was always ice-cream on a Sunday night when we watched the weekend feature movie. I breathe in and smell vanilla. I'm afloat with my memories, in the sea of green.

"The home was left to the two girls."

I jump, returning my focus from my memories to the room. My link to my past becomes a wisp of a memory. Rob's agitation has me on edge and I'm annoyed.

"They didn't know what to do with it."

I rush to get up, feeling like I've been caught out.

"Been empty for almost a year." He picks up a carpet deodoriser sitting on the windowsill. I hadn't noticed it until now. "Need to do something before we open—"

The front door slams shut. The amber beer-bottle divider quivers. Rob drops the deodoriser. The scent of pine fills the air. He looks at the door and back at me. In all these years of working together, he's never looked so pale. He squares his shoulders, adjusts his belt.

"Well, at least it smells a bit better," he says as he puts the container back on the sill. The pile of white powder looks like a mini sand dune. I can't help giggling again.

Rob clears his throat, scuffs the powder. "Better get on with it, then." He leaves white footsteps in a path to the front door. "I think I'll wait outside," Rob says, and pulls the door closed behind him.

"Just you and me, hey?" I say to the house.

It's more intimate now Rob's gone. The clock in the entranceway ticks. A tap drips, but it's not from one of the fixtures I've seen. I clutch my pen and notepad tighter. It doesn't feel like I'm alone.

Focusing on the writing, I continue. *Large lounge; original kitchen, green laminate bench; rooms, good-sized and light-filled. Art Deco?* Umm, not quite. I tap my pen, try to draft something in my head as I walk faster through the house, wanting to finish. *Large linen press. Solid oak polished boards. Bathroom original but clean condition. Three bedrooms, all with BIRs.*

Just one more room to go.

As I approach, the dripping noise slows. The clock's ticks become longer, sluggish. The air thickens, it's harder to breathe. My legs are heavy, as if I'm wading through sludge. Voices, disembodied, compete like an untuned radio between stations. Each beat of my heart is a separate action. The temperature has dropped, goosebumps prick my skin.

The smell of Old Spice and damp woollen blankets fills the air. I take one more step and enter the final room. A vinyl recliner draped in a multicoloured, crotchet rug sits in front of a large window next to a solitary single bed.

He stands beside the chair, ethereal and frail. The carpet in this room is a faded, dirty bile-green, worn and threadbare. My pen falls from shaking fingers and my jaw drops.

He moves to the chair and sits, eyes begging with a question I don't understand, then his body spasms and he's clutching at his throat, struggling to breathe. *Help me*, he mouths.

I back away. The crackle of static fills the room.

Help me, he repeats, needy and insistent. *Help, help meeeeeeeeeeee.*

Waves of voices roll in and join him, banding together – screaming, roaring, wailing – a tsunami of dissent. Then, as it peaks, the wave breaks in a downpour of despair, crashing, crashing against the shore.

And I remember it all.

My father. He was sick. I couldn't help. I was too busy, ignored his calls. He had been drowning too, his lungs filling with fluid. Drowning in his own sea of green.

My notebook is pressed into my stomach, protecting me from pain that's revisited but real. He was so angry and alone, right until the end. We were never able to help him.

"Don't go," dead voices plead, separately and together. I turn away, like—

"—like you did before," they say.

"I'm sorry," I whisper, and run to the door.

Rob's waiting in the carport, but I don't stop. "I'll have it done by tomorrow."

"What about the—?"

"Ring you later."

My car's moving before I've shut the door. Rob runs down the drive, waving, calling out. The car shoots forward, and I'm gripping the wheel to stop my hands from shaking. Emotion wells, grows solid in my throat and all the tears from so long ago are able to release.

———◆———◆———

At home, I sit at my desk. My workspace is where I bring things to life; it's a place I feel safe. Next to my computer is the photo of my sister and me sitting on the carpet in our lounge room, sailing the calm green sea. Dad sits in his recliner in the corner, reading. It was one of the times I loved. I put the photo down and start to type.

The ad writes itself. A quick skim and it's almost done. But something's missing – the line that's the kicker, the one that sells the home.

Then I hear it. A whisper.

"Breathe." My father's voice.

This time I don't run. There is a comfort in his voice. I take the breath he couldn't. And another. A warm hand rests upon my shoulder.

This is what we write:

A loving family home. In need of some attention, and a little TLC.

ᗞARK IN HERE

Stainless steel presses, cold and unforgiving, against my back. It's dark in here, not even a pinprick. And it's so cold. My body feels numb, but the panic grabs at my chest and radiates in waves with nowhere for it to go. "Let me out," I yell.

Doors open and close around me, muffled voices filter through the walls and cut in and out like a radio off station.

A door flings open and light pours in. My body is rolled out. Someone else is rolled out, too. Everything is light. Spectral shapes move around us like white shadows, prodding, listening, checking for life. But I look only at the pale girl. She's young, like me, about twenty-five, a similar build and colouring. Long hair matted black with blood frames deep gashes on her ruined face. There are more lacerations on her ribcage; her right breast is torn off. A wild animal scent lingers in the air. Compared to hers, my body is unblemished, my skin unmarked.

Our gazes lock, then the pale lady blinks.

The spectres come between us. "We've got a live one," one spectre says.

The hospital bed wheels away.

"What about me?" I say to the now-empty room.

Scrunch

I traverse the forest, lost, alone,

silently despairing.

And in the clearing, a frightening sight,

Monsterish and it's… staring.

I run, although not fast enough—

Then its gnawing, scrunching… tearing.

END OF THE LINE

They're handin' out the rations and today my baby's there instead of me. All fourteen years of him. Six-foot-one, skin'n'bone, lanky as an unfed stray, but Davie stands in that line like a pro. Enough to make a mother proud, it is. And maybe, if it all works out, once he grabs those rations—

The klaxon sounds.

"*This is a non-urgent announcement. Gates close in twenty minutes. Get your rations and return to your bunkers.*"

We can leave. Find somethin' better. Anyways, he's near the front. Ten more to go and he'll have the rations. There's a place they say is safe, better. I try and study the map. But I can't stop watchin' him. He's so full of himself, first time in that line. Like a man, he says. Shoulders square, full of sass. He ain't no man yet. But, parents gotta let the young'uns grow. It's tough out there and he's gotta learn.

They say it's pretty bad now. More of 'em come in every day. We dunno where they're from, but they're bad news. Those dark shapes stay fixed in my mind, pictures I seen from when we had the telly. Fear crawls up my spine, for me, for Davie more. I shake my head, move on. Count my blessins instead. Lookin' at my boy, my heart swells big as my backpack. I'm lucky orright.

But in a flash, it changes. The stoopid kid... He's turned around, wavin'. Didn't he listen? I wave back, my arms like windmills. "Turn back," I yell, but he don't hear. Jus' keeps wearin' that goofy grin.

The klaxon sounds.

"*This is a non-urgent announcement. Gates close in fifteen minutes. If you are not in line for rations, return to your bunkers.*"

And when he's turned back, that one step outta line is enough to lose his place. Those men, those wolves, they close the gap like the pack they are.

Like he was never there. He don't even try to get back his spot, my boy ain't no dummy. Well, most times, anyways. Shoulders slouched, despairing, he turns to the back of the line. Then stops, halfways.

"Whatchadoin'!?" I yell. I can see him, but I can't see it all. They're all turning now, lookin' at the fence—

The klaxon sounds.

"*This is not a drill. Return to your bunkers. Return to your—*"

—lookin' at what's left of the fence. Somethin's comin' *through* it. Big shapes on thick legs with huntin' eyes and hungry jaws, just like those shapes on telly, but worse, and they're lookin' at the line like they're the rations. Behind, in front. Everywhere.

"Davie!" I lurch forward, but there ain't nowhere to go. There's a wall of shiftin' fur with barbs of ivory teeth and claws. And lots of blood and—

The piece of paper I'm holdin' drops to the ground. There ain't no escapin' anymore.

The klaxon sounds.

And sounds.

A Stranger With My Face

One thing that's for certain: my kitchen's never been so clean. Every speck and surface, gleaming. The knives glint in the block, shiny, silver, sharp. I cleaned them, too.

I take one out to cut potatoes and catch my reflection in the blade. I don't look like me. Calm and self-assured, not nervous, insecure. My gaze is steady, not timid or looking for somewhere safe.

A car pulls into the drive. It's my son Ben with Lil and Jimmy, right on time.

I keep cutting, thinking about what a lovely quiet Christmas this will be – not like the other ones, poisoned with miserable complaints.

I open the oven and put in the potatoes, letting the smell of roast turkey fill the air. The front door bursts open, and in comes Jimmy, a bundle of five-year-old joy. Jimmy has gifts up to his chin. I point to the Christmas tree, where he lets them cascade down. My tree is already well loaded, and breaks some of the fall. Some of the presents already there will go in the trash once everybody leaves.

I rush over for hugs.

Christmas lights blink on and off – pinpricks of white on green. Red glinting baubles nestle amongst the snowy trim. Poor choice of colours this year. All I see is blood on skin.

My husband really should have been more careful while I was preparing dinner. He took a step too far last night, criticising all of us, saying it would be better if I was gone. I should "go move in with my bloody kid," he said. The nerve. It went on and on, and then he threatened to cancel Christmas. I mean, how could he? It's the one day we're all together. When I said I'd had enough, he hit me! After 35 years of it, I finally said no. It felt good. I said no some more.

I make coffees and get Jimmy a juice. We sit down to unwrap the presents.

"Where's Dad?" Ben asks.

And the stranger in me says, "He's not coming."

They all turn and stare; they must see the stranger, too. Jimmy's looking at my black eye, even though I covered it with makeup.

"Good," says Ben, clasping my hand. Lil puts an arm around my shoulders.

The stranger holds her head up high.

"It's been a long time coming," I say.

They ask no more questions, and we have a lovely day.

When everyone has left, there's the sudden quiet of the house. No complaining. No aggression. Lights blink on and off, sending weird shadows round the room.

Did I do those things? Was it really me? I don't believe it, though the evidence lays it bare. The freshly dug soil, the shovel against the shed. The lingering smell of bleach.

I still can't believe what I did with those knives.

Fertiliser. That's what he is now. Tomorrow I'll buy a lemon tree. I bet he'll nurture it just fine. I think if he was here, he'd want to complain about that, too.

MEASURE

"Fascinating," says the doctor.
"Fast-moving necrosis! If I can measure how long it
takes to reach the brain—"
The patient bites his arm.
"Not long," I say, and run.

BROKEN

Is it real? Who can say? Each time I touch you, I forget. Forget you are not whole.

Love has its own master. Why must I torture myself so?

Brown eyes, like a chasm. I dive in. Kiss your willing lips, taste desire. Hints of champagne, chocolate, promises of more. Pulling back, I tuck a loose hair behind your ear, trail red painted nails down your neck. Skin soft, silken. Almost…

A burst of pheromones. I'm going down, further down. Your hands explore my neck, my breasts. Desire licks my clit. The warmth spreads.

I control it. Tease your tender buds with my tongue. Hands in my hair pull me close.

That's the trigger. I've lost control.

I kiss your neck, frantic, fast. Nipples, pebbles on our chests. A moan, a whimper, a plea. My tongue finds yours. We blend together. A hand slips between my legs. You know exactly what to do.

I try to return the favour, but only find your cold, metal edge.

I'm forced to remember what you are, what I've done.

"Sleep," I command.

Your artificial light dims. You still.

I cry.

My memory bursts forth – the fit of rage. Your missing half, twisted metal and fake skin. Broken. Detritus by the bed.

I tell myself that it was never really love.

SPARKLE

"Add an incisor glint, a twinkle in your eye?" said Elvira.

"Too sparkly?" Vlad was an old-school vampire.

"Modern."

Reluctantly, Vlad admitted this Tinder profile now captured his inner glow.

A Warm Embrace

Ivana crept past the dark room, not wanting to wake her parents. The last thing she needed was another lecture about going out in the daytime. Last time she went out in the afternoon they assaulted her at the front door with their annoying words of wisdom.

"Daytime is for the living!" said Gregor, her father. "Honour your ancestors!"

And, from her mother, "Try to stay out of the sunlight, Ivana. You don't want to get a human tan!"

She wasn't like them. Would never be like them. Not now, not ever.

Ivana made it halfway down the stairs before her mother appeared from nowhere at the front door. Ivana knew she'd be able to do that too when she turned. She thought it was a cool trick, but she'd never let her mother know. Ivana put extra effort into looking unimpressed.

"Going out?" her mother, Camille, said.

The sigh she'd been holding in finally escaped. "Yes, Camille." She'd used their first names for years, especially enjoying when her parents flinched at the lack of respect.

Long and gleaming ivory canines became visible as Camille's lips curled with distaste. "Are you going to meet… him?"

"His name is Vic, *Camille*, and what is it to you anyway?"

"Are you going to keep him once you turn, do you think?

Humans can be quite handy to have around, especially for doing things during the day."

Ivana shot her a glare so cold an ice queen would have been proud.

"Okay," said Camille, "I was just asking." But she didn't move. "You've had something to eat? You don't want to be hungry when you're out. You're at the age now, and anything can bring on the change. It is daytime, and once you turn, you know it's the end of these" – she waved a dismissive hand at the door – "day trips."

Ivana knew full well. She may have been born human, but she had their ancient blood in her veins. They'd told her ever since she was twelve years old that her humanness would end once the change arrived, and now puberty and her hormones were in full swing, she could feel it was coming soon. Her life would change as soon as she drank blood and Ivana would become just like *them*. She'd asked her mother once if she could just stay human, forever. Camille had laughed. "We are high born!" she'd declared. "There's a pecking order, Ivana, and we're at the top. You cannot fight your nature."

Camille stroked Ivana's long, dark hair. "Plus, sweet girl, you don't want to turn during the day, because, well, we all know what happens then."

Ivana remembered the accounts of when Aunt Beatrice had turned during the day. Quite the spectacle, they'd said. The second she'd stepped into the sunlight after feeding, she practically exploded. The Australian newspaper reports had called it a verified case of madness and spontaneous combustion. But it was in 1915, seven years before the release of *Nosferatu*, so there wasn't a lot of focus on what else it might have been at the time. If it wasn't for the framed newspaper cutting on the wall, Ivana might have thought it was a family myth to scare her.

Camilla sniffed and looked displeased. "Is it that time of the…?"

Ivana rolled her eyes, reaching for the door.

"You know, vampire urges are heightened when you are…" Her mother looked downwards. After all these centuries of being alive, her mother still couldn't speak about periods.

"Don't go out, Ivana. You are almost sixteen. You need to think of your future, finding a proper mate, keeping our line alive. We can find you a suitor. I can call the Badeauxs in France, or, somewhere closer, the Baccucis in Alice Springs." A look of excitement crossed her mother's face. "If you get pregnant now, before you change, it will be a much easier birth. Remember, Gregor, how we had to use a surrogate and—"

The conversation had gone from periods to life-long commitment and children, and Ivana wasn't ready. She'd never be ready.

"It's a sunny day today," Ivana said, a thinly veiled threat. "You better move or – do you remember Cousin Beatrice?!" Ivana yanked open the door. Camille retreated with a hiss; a small whiff of smoke from singed skin following in her wake. Gregor was nowhere to be seen.

As Ivana walked, suburban living filled her senses. Mowers hummed across lawns, the scents of grass clippings and salty sweat wafted by on the breeze. Sun shone brightly overhead, warming her back. She smiled at Mr Henderson as she passed him washing his Prius in his driveway. He smiled and nodded back. The roller-blading twins from number 35 came speeding past on the pavement with a wave and a hello, almost knocking her over. Bikes, skateboards, and people. Sunlight, warm and comforting. Birds in chorus in the trees. She drank it all in. Cars on the road, spring music in the air. It was the world she loved. She wanted to stay like this forever.

Her mother's words cut through her joy. *There is no coming back once you change.*

Ivana blocked her out and turned the corner. Vic was waiting at the park, by his mum's Corolla. He leaned against the car, a juxtaposition of distinctiveness again the banality of everyday, like a Banksy artwork. All black leather and piercings, a pale complexion. He was made for night, but not in the same way as her. *Never* like her.

"Hey, babe," Vic said, welcoming her in a deep, passionate embrace. He tasted of cigarettes, and something else she wasn't sure of. Something new. Copper, iron. It was earthy. Delicious.

Her pulse quickened.

She gently pushed Vic, and those thoughts, away.

Vic studied her face. "You look different today." He threaded strands of her hair behind her ear.

"In what way?" she asked.

"More beautiful?"

Ivana laughed. "Con artist."

Vic reached past her to open the car door, but Ivana shook her head. "It's such a beautiful day. Let's walk through the park. Cut across the bridge." She'd always liked the water. "How long until the movie starts?"

Vic fished around in his pocket and pulled out the tickets. "In an hour. Plenty of time." The tickets were for Cinema Europa, which meant a foreign film. Probably something smutty, knowing him. Ivana raised an eyebrow. "What's the flick?"

Vic grinned, broad and infectious, and slipped his warm hand into hers. It felt so warm. He felt so… *alive.*

"*Let the Right One In,*" he replied. "Something a bit different."

Ivana hadn't heard of it. At least it wasn't another *Iron Man* or *Scary Movie.* Whatever. She just enjoyed being with him. While they both lived with their parents, the cinema gave them a private place to go.

"It's a celebration day today," Vic said. "Maybe we can go to dinner after?"

"What are we celebrating?" Ivana asked. Vic never had any money.

"Remember that game I made, where the characters—"

A young girl ran past, brushing against Ivana. She smelled of cherry vanilla and something else. Those same strange hints of copper when she'd kissed Vic.

"Sorry," said the girl, picking up a nearby ball. She was a small thing, about eight, and the mass of hair framed a freckled face. Cute. *And delicious,* Ivana thought.

"Are you okay?" asked Vic.

"I think so," Ivana said, but the scent lingered in the air. Hints of vanilla cherry, and hints of copper.

Around her and Vic, families sat on blankets with picnic baskets in the park. Walking past them, Ivana thought of her own mother and father, only ever able to come out at night. She'd had a nanny around for the day things, but it hadn't been the same. She felt miserable.

Vic was chatting away about his game in the background,

but she couldn't get out of her own thoughts. Her emotions seemed deeper, sadder even, and her senses sharper, more acute. The air was alive as it brushed her face. She knew the exact direction of the wind, where it had come from and the lands it had blown through. Where birdsong had been a chorus a moment earlier, she now heard individual voices. The grass, spongy underfoot, gave way to the incessant activity of insects underground. Was she imagining these things? Was this because of her period, or was it because she was getting ready to change?

She was cross at her mother all over again for not explaining this to her, instead just trying to coax her to a vampire way of life.

As they neared the bridge, the sound of running water, normally a balm to a troubled mood, did little to shift it; she imagined floating on her back, being carried away.

"Earth to Ivana!"

Ivana came back with a shock. She'd lost any sense of where she was. "Sorry, Vic. I-I—"

"You haven't heard a word, have you?" Anger flashed, then his demeanour softened. "Family stuff again?"

It was easier to just say yes. She nodded. "Tell me again, will you?" she said, squeezing his hand.

"Okay. But listen this time!"

Vic was so excited. She loved his passion and zest for life.

"Ivana, they gave me an advance! They liked my game design. But not only that, I've signed a contract to deliver three more. I have a job, Ivana. A real, paying job. We can finally get a place together. You don't have to live with your parents anymore."

It was what she'd wanted for ages. But what if she was changing? It would never happen.

"Oh, that's brilliant, Vic!" She hid her concerns in a hug. "I knew you could do it." Leaning over the rail of the bridge, she said, "When does it start?"

She stared into the water, burdened by a million problems. Would he want to convert, to live like her? To feed on the lifeforce of others? Would her parents accept him if he did? Would she be able to live like this? All she'd wanted was to be with him, to be *like* him. Now it all seemed so complicated.

Ivana's reflection looked back at her from the water. She was pale, too pale. The sun could never give her a rosy glow like she'd seen on that child. Her floral dress hung on her like cheerful drapes in a dreary room – a false facade of brightness. If she dressed in black, she'd look like Morticia Addams.

As she stared into the lake, the water reflected her worst fears. She saw a vision of herself changed. Her teeth grown into fangs, and her skin paled further. Next to her, Vic's image dulled, and he became a formless shape that housed a strong, beating heart. A blood sack. Ivana broke into a cold sweat.

"—Ivana?"

Vic was holding her. She hadn't even felt him.

"You looked like you were going to faint!"

When she turned to face him, all she could see was a shape, and the veins like little rivers under his skin. She closed her eyes tightly and when she opened them it was Vic again.

"I need to go home now," Ivana said, struggling to stand.

Vic didn't let her go. "If we live together, you're going to have to talk to me about what's going on for you. I know you have trouble at home, and you won't let me come to see you, but it's going to have to stop."

She loved him and loved his strength. A warmth filled her. He made her feel like it could all be okay. She burst into tears, and he held her close.

"Come on," he said. "Let's get to the cinema and we can talk more after the movie."

Against her better judgement, she let him guide her away.

Vic picked seats at the back, as usual. His arm was draped across her shoulders, and she'd nestled in against his collarbone. This was all just the normal routine. She felt secure, safe. They made the most of the opening advertisements by focusing on each other. Like lovers long parted catching up on lost time, their bodies were close and their hands exploring. They earned a few strange looks from scattered patrons, but for the most part they contained themselves. The lights eventually dimmed, and the feature started. Ivana ran a hand down Vic's chest, and he moved it away. "We have to read the subtitles on this one, Ivana. I really want to see this movie."

Ivana tried another kiss, but Vic was determined.

"Subtitles," he said.

Ivana sat back, sulking and disappointed, and picked up the popcorn instead. But in a moment, she too was transfixed. The movie wasn't what she'd expected at all. The characters were just kids. And it all held a huge sense of foreboding.

"Vic?" She moved in closer, unsure if she was terrified or excited. On the screen, a male character strung up a young boy and, without any great ceremony, slit his throat. *She could smell the blood.* She stiffened against Vic.

Vic tried to sooth her. "It's okay. I probably should have said it was a horror."

Ivana barely heard him, her focus fully on the film, on the thick, viscous fluid pouring out, the fear she imagined the dying boy felt. She was right there, drinking that blood. Her senses sharpened even further. She smelled the Old Spice on the man in the second row, and on his partner, Bella Rosa by Oscar De La Renta. And her eyesight! Every pixel on the big screen was acute and clear, both separate and together.

This feeling was like a drug. A groan of longing escaped her lips.

"Well okay, then," Vic said, drawing her closer. "But later."

And beside her, all she could hear was the steady kerthump of Vic's heart, and all she could smell were the luscious earthy scents—

Hints of copper, iron, earth. More than hints, a wave.

Lust, longing and—

Oh, the need!

—his blood! Flowing, pulsing, thick as honey, and just as sweet.

And then she was taking, taking it all.

"Ivana!" Vic tried to push her away, but she held tight. Her new razor-sharp incisors had found his jugular. She clamped one hand over his mouth while the other held him close, and she was biting, drinking, sucking. Until Vic was almost empty and still.

Awareness returned in a different rush. What had she done? A sob came from deep within, stifled at the last as she looked around to see if others had seen what she had done. They all looked forward, watching the horror unfolding on the screen instead.

She let Vic go, gently placing him back in his seat. Clotted, sticky wetness soaked her clothes, her skin. She sat back, bereft, heartbroken, but more alive than she'd ever felt.

Vic's head lolled back, eyes glazed and staring at the ceiling. He was dead. Blood made his dull leather jacket a shiny patent black. What a terrible mess! There'd be no future for them now. She ran a hand across his cheek, tears streaming down her face.

A future unfolded in her mind. One without Vic. One inside, now, with *them*. Her mother's words, the tie that binds. *Once you feed…*

"Oh, Vic," she whispered, her lip trembling. She drew him close for their final embrace.

Gathering herself, Ivana closed Vic's eyes and tilted him to the side. He looked peacefully asleep, not dead. When the lights came on, of course, his body would tell a truer story. She took his jacket to cover some of the blood splatter on her own clothes, wiping the excess onto his jeans. She sat back and watched the rest of the movie, nibbling at the blood-soaked popcorn, waiting for the sun to set so she could leave safely.

She felt the change creep across her. Each moment brought with it a difference: a physical strengthening, her worries falling away. She was becoming more *herself,* somehow than she'd ever been.

And, the movie, well, it was pretty good, really. She was glad she'd come to see it.

She left the cinema as soon as the credits started to roll. As she neared the exit it was a great relief to see the sun had set. As she opened the door to the night, screams and fear followed behind.

She could feel the fear as a tangible thing. The feeling was divine! Ivana lingered a moment out of sight in the park to enjoy the scene. But poor Vic. She had really loved him. Poor, poor *delicious* Vic. She pictured his dead eyes, forever without another spark. A tear fell down her cheek – or at least, she felt like a tear should fall down her cheek. She no longer had functioning tear ducts.

Ivana smiled. The benefits of being undead seemed to be growing rather quickly. A car went past, full of more delicious, sweaty testosterone-fuelled bodies, and one of the boys whistled. She took a breath, long and deep, drawing in the whistler's particular scent. She'd follow that one up later.

For the first time in her life, Ivana was looking forward to going home. It was finally time to have that unbeating heart-to-heart with Mother.

Her future looked dark and wonderous.

HE SAID
THERE'D BE CHICKS

Benny only came on this camping trip because Jock said there'd be beer and chicks. Turned out there was beer, but no chicks. When Benny asked where they were, Jock said to be patient, the chicks would come later. But three hours and lots of beers later, still nothing.

It was fun at first, sneaking away from home to do something he wasn't allowed to. They'd set up camp, cooked stew over the campfire, had a beer, talked a lot of shit. But then Benny had started to feel sick. He didn't know if it was the mushrooms Jock had added to the stew, or anxiety kicking in. Being deep in the bush, you couldn't even hear cars on the highway. And his phone: not a single bar of range. How would anyone find them, anyway?

At some point after dinner, things changed. Subtle things, like Jock stopping talking, and started doing disconcerting things like making strange twitching movements and clicking noises. Benny downed another beer while he figured out what to do. Jock was getting weirder by the minute. Maybe the mushrooms had been funny. It would explain a lot.

Benny had only started hanging out with Jock recently, after they'd met online. Sure, Jock was much older, but they liked all the same things: gaming, beer, chicks. When Jock had invited him on this overnight camp, he'd initially wondered why, but it hadn't taken long to warm to the idea. There'd be chicks. At fifteen, most things were about chicks.

But now Benny wanted to go home. He didn't want to say it, though, because he didn't want to be uncool. After this beer, he decided he'd pack up his shit, sneak off and hitchhike home.

"Hey, Jock," he said. "Want a cold one?"

Jock twitched, but there was no sign he'd heard. The way the campfire lit his face made him look super creepy; his eyes black and beady, his nose beak-like and protruding. A chill wind raised goosebumps on Benny's bare arms. Shit was getting *too* weird. What a dumbass he was to have come along.

Before Benny had reached the esky, an unpleasant burning stench wafted past him. It smelled like—

"Jock!" Benny forgot the beer and grabbed Jock's arm out of the fire. "What are you doing?"

Jock's fingers were a nasty shade of red and black, and still smoking. Bile rose in Benny's throat, mingling with the charcoal smell in the air. Gagging, he rushed to the esky and scooped up handfuls of ice. When he put the ice on Jock's hand, the flesh was so hot it sizzled. Benny could see exposed bone.

Jock turned towards Benny and smiled. "Thanks, man."

Benny's stomach flipped. Jock's face looked wrong. Perhaps it was the firelight throwing shadows. Benny blinked a few times, but Jock still looked like—

A searing pain flared in Benny's hand. He staggered to his seat. The burning smell was closer. What the fuck? Benny's hand sat in his lap, a charred mess of swollen digits.

"Benny," Jock said.

Jock stood back from the fire, almost in the dark. From what Benny could see, he looked even more bird-like now. His nose was a long beak, and his unburnt hands were sprouting talons from the nails. Jock drew a talon across his chest and grinned.

The cut appeared on Benny's chest instead, blood soaking his t-shirt.

Benny started to cry.

"Neat trick, huh?" Jock clucked. "Magic. And it wasn't the mushrooms in the stew, in case you're wondering."

Two young girls appeared next to him. They twittered with excitement as one picked up his burnt hand and started to nibble on a finger.

Benny screamed and screamed. The girls beside him grew beaks and sprouted feathers.

"And the fire," said Jock, between whistles and clucks. "We like our meat roasted."

The last thing Benny heard before he slipped away was Jock, proclaiming in a voice that slowed and slurred like a recording playing at half speed, "See, I told you there'd be chicks."

CONFINEMENT

Ana wasn't sure what would kill her first: the virus or the boredom.

The ticking of the clock on the mantle was too loud, the book, one she'd read before. Frustration settled like a coat on a summer's day, heavy and unwanted. It had been the same routine for weeks: get up, eat breakfast, read, dress in protective gear, pick up rations, come home, disinfect and wash everything, and then work out what they could cook for dinner with what they'd been given.

Nine a.m. and the day stretched uninvitingly ahead. She groaned inwardly. If John heard her complain he'd be over with some message of positivity. It was all driving her nuts.

Ana put the book aside. It wasn't a reading day today. She flicked on the radio. The blandness of government-selected soft jazz filled the room. Like everyone else, she'd relied on streaming services rather than retaining a library of movie DVDs or music CDs. When they'd rerouted comms to essential use only, she'd lost it all.

John stood in the kitchen, wearing boxers, reading an old sports magazine. He leant against the bench, oblivious to the burnt-toast smoke pluming around him.

"John, the—"

He yanked the cord, shorting the toaster and the rest of the power.

Yelling immediately started in the apartment to the left.

Then, a crash on the right. The whole floor must be out. A thump above, more yells and slamming doors.

Maybe a few floors.

"Sorry, love." He held up black toast.

"It's okay," she lied, trying to hide brimming tears. He was such a klutz. She took a deep breath, stretched, and walked to the balcony. Below, she saw the usual soldiers, spaced along the road to keep order. Besides the army and the few people scuttling about to collect rations, the streets were barren. Not even pets scampered anymore. If your pet got out, it would disappear immediately to top up food supply.

Something fell from above. If she'd been hanging out over the rail, as she often did, it would have hit her. She heard the familiar splat on the pavement four floors below and knew exactly what it was. She stepped back, not needing to see.

John was over in a moment, his arms around her, crying. "I hate this. Hate it so goddamn much."

Ana held him close, afraid if she said a word she'd unravel, too. Maybe things could be worse.

Choppers beat the air overhead.

"It's the trial vaccine," she said.

John released her slightly, wiped his eyes. "Hope it works this time."

The air outside thickened pink and smoky with chemicals. It reminded her of a distant memory of a Cary Grant in *North by Northwest*, where he'd been running to escape a crop duster. Crop dusting – only now they were people dusting.

Would the world ever return to any sort of normal? Another question she was scared to voice. The choppers receded to a distant hum.

The lights flickered. Someone must have fixed the fuse. In a burst of static, the radio lurched on.

"Hey, someone must have replaced the—"

"Shh," she said. Urgent voices had replaced the jazz.

"Repeat, do not—" Transmission was intermittent.

"Fix it, John!"

John was already adjusting the settings.

"Repeat. Close your windows. Do not—" A high pitch squeal erupted, then the radio went silent. The lights stayed on, so this time it wasn't the power.

A pink mist invaded the room.

The sound of gunfire and car alarms filled the streets outside. Something thudded against her balcony – no, onto it. She nestled tightly against John's chest. She couldn't look. He held her tight. Too tight—

Why couldn't she feel a heartbeat? He growled. Everything went black.

The radio spluttered on. The only music, the meaningless sound of black static.

DRIFT

The orange glow sinks below the horizon.

Cicadas serenade.

Stars flicker, fall and blink out.

We know the sun won't rise, but our wishes drift, seeking

birdsong and sunny mornings.

The Beating of
Her Heart

In my house all I can hear is the beating of her heart.
It's in the walls, and through the halls… and it's tearing me apart.

Two weeks ago she left me for some fancy bureaucrat.
She took the car, the bank account – she even took the cat.

Did she think that I would take it, that I'd let her get away?
That she was boss, and called the shots, and had the final say?

There's no way I'd allow her to leave me with this pain.
I sought her out to bring her here so we'd be together again.

My plan met with refusal; insistence things were ended.
I said they weren't until *I* said… things broken must be mended.

Chloroformed, I took her home, ignored her mock resistance.
If she'd only been compliant! She just couldn't go the distance.

It was her fault that she struggled, fell down the flight of stairs
and bashed her head and bled and bled…
till brains became her hair.

And it's her fault all this happened, because if she'd never strayed,
she'd still be here, we'd be a pair… and there wouldn't be a grave.

I buried her in the garden, thinking this would be her end.
But it was not, and she remains, a most unwelcome friend.

At night I hear her moaning: sighs, laments, and cries of woe.
In death she speaks much more than life, and I can't
force her to go!

In my house all I can hear is the beating of her heart.
It's in the walls, and through the halls… and it's tearing me apart.

A Shadow in This Red Rock

I'd told myself that the next funeral after Mother's would be my own – but I'd not imagined anything like this. I'm shackled, stuck. I watch from a distance, unable to say my final words to you, or about you.

They gather around the casket, the scatter of mourners. We didn't have many friends. The sun is bright and strong. Birds sing in the trees. You would say there's no room for joy in death. Funerals should be fast and over – life is for the living, and the dead are for the worms.

Your mother watches on, resentment seething like a noxious cloud. She doesn't want to be here, to say these last goodbyes.

I see through a miasma of red. Think about what led us here. Memory takes me home.

***

The red rock sits upon the windowsill above the sink. It is smaller and slightly rounder than an egg, the colour of dried blood, its texture smooth, shiny and deep. It looks like an agate, but colours shift underneath the surface like viscous oil. Dawn had found it among her mother's things, when she'd been looking at photos, in an old tin she'd almost chucked out. When she'd picked it up, she was surprised to find it warm. She'd held it to her chest and closed her eyes, and an image of her mother appeared. The rock's warmth enveloped her, immediately connecting to her heart.

It's here so she can see it every day. When the light strikes it a certain way, red splinters beam around the room. Faceted rubies bloom bright and exquisite on walls and peeling laminates, lifting their damaged and dirty creams. On the black-and-white chequered lino, rusty red diamonds blink on and off. Stunning, how such a small rock has such a mesmerising effect.

Dawn rinses her coffee cup and stares into its depths. Glimpses of her childhood screen in her mind: her innocent unlined face sun-darkened and dust-painted, red dirt from top to toenail, her mother at work in the homestead kitchen. Playing tiggy with the other children, laughing, fearless: You're it! When the time came for Dawn and her mother to move on, and the owners at the homestead said goodbye, one of the children gave Mother the rock. A keepsake. A good wish for future travels. That stay at the homestead was as close to a family home as Dawn had ever known.

She clings to this feeling, because after that lurks deeper, darker things.

Family.

Whisper-soft, the word nudges inside her mind, like a distant echo. It is close and far, familiar and strange.

Murderer.

A sharp intake of breath. Are the words from her memory, or the rock?

"Hey, Dawn, whatchalookin' at?" says Pete.

She jumps. Hadn't even heard him come downstairs. She turns around. He's already at the table, already focusing elsewhere, his attention deserting her at the first chance.

"Coffee?" she asks.

"I don't have to be at work until ten. How 'bout you cook

me a big brekky?" he says.

Dawn plans to meet Carly at nine to talk about a part-time job offer. It's already after eight. She isn't sure Pete will be happy about her working, so she doesn't say anything.

"Too busy?" says Pete, words loaded.

"No, not at all," says Dawn, smiling, mentally putting the appointment aside. She'll deal with it later.

By the time Pete finishes his sausages and bacon big eat – she really spoils him – it is almost ten. She rings Carly and apologises, but Carly isn't having any of it. Cool on the phone, she says maybe it isn't a good idea to mix business and friendship after all. Dawn feels the opportunity sliding out from under her, wondering if it is just as well because of Pete. Hanging up, she feels sadness threatening to swallow her. She pushes the feeling aside and starts cleaning the house, making it spotless. If only the dirty corners and blemishes in her own life could be so easily scrubbed away.

For the moment, she forgets the rock is even there.

I think about you and us. Were you different when we started out? More loving? Less hateful? Were you always the same?

Or was it me?

Was I always destined to walk my mother's path?

There's no answer now. Your mother's eyes hold a hateful glare. They say you deserved more than this life, deserved more than me. It was always me. I was never any good for you. Her contempt reaches across the divide. It is a living, breathing thing.

It's past five in the afternoon when Dawn sits down with another coffee, the house now eucalyptus fresh and not a speck on any surface. Even though it's clean, she can do nothing to fix the patched-up holes in walls, the water-soaked bulging of laminate benchtops and the heaviness of her heart that hangs in the air.

On the windowsill, the rock reflects the rays of the setting sun. Barbs of red light frolic in familiar shapes: rubies, garnets, blood diamonds, on an imperfect palette.

The front door slams shut. 'Honey, I'm home,' says Pete, a laugh following his own private joke.

Dread inches up her back. He's in *that* sort of mood – he's already visited the pub. A few drinks this early usually means trouble into the evening. Almost unconsciously, her hand touches the scar under her left eye, the one from last time. Then it takes only a moment to forget, to bury it again. Her face dons the mask her mother showed her how to wear, the one that says, "happiness is what you make it". She turns towards Pete's voice. "I'm in the kitchen, Pete. Are you home for dinner?"

He walks upstairs without reply. That means he's probably going out again. She puts a chopping board on the bench and pulls out the vegetables. As she cuts, she thinks about the missed meeting with Carly, telling herself she wouldn't have liked the job. Cleaning other peoples' houses is not so exciting a prospect, and besides, she's got enough to do cleaning their house. And when the baby comes – she rubs her belly, which at eight weeks isn't even showing – she'll be even busier at home.

After she is done, she rinses the knife. Stainless steel catches the rock's light and glints of bloody red trigger something else from a time before. She falls under the spell. A new memory scratches the surface now, one she's tried hard to forget.

Doctor. Doctor!

The words fill her with alarm.

Sirens scream. Blue and red lights bounce off the walls. Ambulance officers prepare her mother for hospital. Her stepdad has fled, is nowhere in sight. Mother's face is bruised, bloody, her right eye puffed shut. A trickle of blood escapes her ear.

A bad fall, she says at the hospital, though no one believes it. The officer asks Dawn questions, but there are no answers she wants to give while her mother shakes a subtle *no*. The police suspect her stepfather, but there'll never be any proof. The doctor says Mother's next "fall" might be her last, while side-eying Dawn. Mother looks the other way. Says she'll be more careful.

Another endless loop.

Do we have to become our parents? Repeat all their mistakes? Questions swirl in my head, too late to change events. Could we have changed who we were?

You never asked these things. You said life was what you made it — you had to show it who was boss. Your mother used to nod when you said this. In her eyes, you were always right.

A searing pain shoots down Dawn's finger, bringing her right back to her sullied kitchen. She drops the knife. Blood streams, swirling with the tap water in the sink. She sees the white of bone.

"Oh, nasty cut," says Pete, planting a kiss on her cheek, and giving her a small squeeze. It reminds her of happier days, walks on the beach and the promise of shared dreams. Then Dawn flinches. He smells of cologne and a pending night out. "I think I need stitches," she says.

Pete grabs a beer from the fridge, sits at the kitchen table. "You'll be right. Just chuck on a band-aid."

Dawn goes to the bathroom for bandages. Behind her, Pete doesn't let up. "You're leaving a trail of blood, Dawn!"

Her instincts are to apologise, but she holds the "sorry" in. Buries it.

Even as she finishes bandaging, tiny blood-roses bloom. She grabs a cloth, hoping the bandage holds until she's finished cleaning up. Pete sucks on his beer while she gets on her knees to wipe blood from the floor.

"I'm going out tonight. It's a work thing, with the boys."

Dawn looks up at him. He has a glint in his eye, one not matching his words. Tonight she'll be smelling a nameless woman's musky perfume when he gets home.

Lies. Lies!

The rock's words bounce around her head.

"Over there, you missed a bit," he says.

Dawn pushes down her scream. She wishes he'd just get out. Go. *Go!*

"What did you say?" Pete says.

Did she say it out loud? She doesn't think so. "I didn't say anything, Pete!" She stands up, takes the bloodied cloth to the sink.

On the sill, the red rock gleams brighter. Bloodshot light seeps out from its depths. A red miasma reaches into the room.

Murderer, murderer!

Did she say the words?

"What the hell, Dawn?"

"It isn't me. It's the rock!"

"Christ. Talking rocks. Yeah, right. I think the pregnancy is fucking with your mind. Just shut up. Get me another beer."

Dawn doesn't move. Pete raises a hand and she flinches.

"Useless…" he says, opening the fridge.

Pete sits back down at the table with a second beer, shaking his head. "You sayin' no now, too? Is the rock sayin' it as well?" He sniggers. "You know what happened to your mum when she said no."

She wishes she'd never told him about it, fighting back tears. "You don't love me," says Dawn, in the smallest voice, her mother's voice. "Or the baby."

Pete loosens his tie. Takes a long slug of amber brew. "You know, I take some time to be with you, and all you have is these pathetic stories and complaints."

She's crossed the invisible line on the elusive yet well-worn track. A part of her retreats, knowing what comes next.

He stands abruptly and the chair flies back into the fridge with a loud clang. The short distance between them disappears in a blink. Bone crunches as his right fist hits her cheek, then his left hits her jaw. He pulls back, as if realising what he's done. But looking at her split lip only seems to make him angrier, and in a second his hands are around her throat.

"Respect. Not too much to ask for? What sort of a fucking mother are you going to be anyway?"

He shoves Dawn harder against the sink.

A maelstrom of red light spins around the kitchen, then sucks back into the rock. The red rock screams.

Hurt!

It hurts!

Pete lets go, looks at the rock, colour draining from his face. Dawn gasps for air. He pushes her aside and hurries past. "I'm outta here," he says, not looking back.

The pastor reads the sermon, surrendering your remains to the earth. A dark cloud crosses the sun. It's going to rain. Your mother sneers in the distance. Her anger breathes. It's my fault we are here.

Dawn takes his seat at the table holding the coolness of his beer against the least tender parts of her battered, throbbing face. Her finger has finally stopped bleeding. She'll have to see about her cheekbone, though. This time it might be fractured. Tears slide down her cheeks as she wonders what excuse she'll give the hospital.

Codeine reduces the pain and shock, as does drinking Pete's beer. She finishes one, moves on to the next. Yeah, what sort of a mother will she be?

Another memory cuts through, forgotten yet fresh and familiar: a summer breeze blowing through a different kitchen window, ruffling her mother's white lace curtains. The scent of native jasmine filling the room. Orange, yellow and green flowers wallpapered on kitchen walls, now tinged with streaks of red. Puddles and splashes spoiling her mother's spotless kitchen. Her stepdad looking ten feet tall, towering over Mother as she lies crumpled against cream cupboards, his shoulders rising and falling, fists clenched, screaming at Mother for what she'd made him do. Mother's eyes staring, forever somewhere else.

Dawn had run, then, as far as she could go. She found out later her stepfather went to prison and died there. A small relief, but not justice. The loss gaped again – red raw, poignant, painful.

Dawn is still at the table hours later, sitting in the dark. The rock is silent, its red aura deathly still. Four more empty bottles of his beer now nest in the bin. He'll be really pissed off now.

"Murderer, murderer!" Dawn says the words like a curse, angry at the rock, angry at Pete, angry at everything.

The front door slams. "Honey, I'm home," says Pete, contempt lacing his few slurred words. The familiar dread inches up her back. A chaser of scorching anger follows.

The red rock pulses, slow and steady like a heartbeat. Shades of glowing ruby shift around the walls of the darkened room.

Fuck wearing the mask.

She turns towards Pete's voice. "I'm in the kitchen, Pete. Have you had dinner?"

Removing the sharpest knife from the block, she goes to say hello.

⸻◆◆⸻

Is that you, casting a shadow over this time and place, from wherever you have gone? Rain falls from the sky as you are lowered to your rest. You must be pleased the heavens have bowed to your control, and it's no longer a nice day.

Your mother's dam has broken. Venom gushes from her serpent's tongue, she says your blood is on my hands.

Of course, she is right.

My cuffs chafe as I'm moved, the guard telling me it's over, time to go. I smile, thinking of my mother and her mask, and how my early years served me better than I realised. I tell my unborn child that we will not repeat. That no one will hurt us anymore.

I own it now. I accept what I've become.

Murderer.

The red rock was me all along. It was always me.

⒟ROPLETS

You lay supine, helpless. Supplicant. Complicit in the circumstances creating your demise. Droplets, each a deadly poison, on the way into your veins. I administer the death blow, but only as a penance.

I watch the toxins mix with plasma. Adjust the IV drip. Let it flow.

As the poison drips down the feeder tube, you watch too. Who'd have thought there would be anything we'd willingly experience together? You are bandaged head to toe, unable to talk or move, a hell unto itself. That car accident almost finished you, but not quite. I wonder if watching me meter out this punishment is worse for you, or a sign of sweet release?

Either way, it's a release for me.

The first drop enters your system. You react with widened eyes. I smile, lay a comforting hand on your immobile wrist. "There, there, Daddy. It will be our little secret, won't it?"

Your panic sets in. As the poison seeps, I inject more venom with my words. "Remember how I always begged you to stop?"

Your eyes plead.

I tenderly stroke your cheek. "Begged you to stop."

Muscles contract. Tighten. You must be in pain.

I slow the feed.

Drink your fear. Savour your agony.

Breath in your life as it leaves you.

The monitor squeals an alert.

The hospital staff rush in and I lament my well-practiced grief.

Mistakes

I open the door to a sea of outstretched palms, beckoning for futures told. They reach closer, clawing, crowding, claustrophobic. "I am Bianca, not Selena," I say, using my own palms as barriers to push through. These parties are always the same.

"Good for business," Selena says. "Lots of fortunes to be told – and made."

I think of what fortunes I'd read them if it were me. I'd tell of impending deaths and scenes of doom. Dead pets, illnesses, betrayals. I'd make them afraid and still take their money. That's what I'd call fun. Their need for constant assurance sickens me. Fortunes. Bah! My fortune is to no longer share a house with my twin, and we'll go our separate ways. I'd almost saved enough.

I turn into the kitchen and close the door, leaving the people on the other side complaining and unsatisfied. A man reaches from behind, close, intimate, his palm hot and wanting on my arm. I turn and he is smiling. He moves in closer, a heat between us. He smells of rum and coconut. Suntan oil or pina coladas? For a moment I am at the beach, on holiday with my lover, Rob.

But this isn't Rob. His hand moves down my arm, slow, sensual. My skin prickles, a heat rises. He has a glint in his eye hinting at past favours.

Selena is a woman of many favours.

I step away, show him the rose tattoo above my heart. Selena doesn't have one of these. "We may look the same," I say, "but I'm not her."

Confusion creases his brow, but he desists. Shrugs. "Okay, maybe later," he says, and leaves.

I look for my sister. Why has she left all these strangers alone in our home? I walk upstairs to my room, away from the party below. His touch lingers on my skin, not unpleasant after all. Hints of things not mine, forbidden summer dreams.

I burst into her room, ready to yell. She isn't here. I pick up her crystal ball, take it with me as I search. For some reason it is calming, like a cold drink on a hot day. The ball grows heavy as I walk, and warm. Maybe I feed it with my wrath.

The sooner I am out of here…

I open my bedroom door and Selena and Rob are in my bed. "What the actual fuck…?"

Rob jumps up, desire retreating. "Bianca?" he says. He looks at Selena, confused. She laughs. He comes towards me. "I can explain…"

Sure, more words. This is not the first time he has strayed.

A vision assails me as I clutch the crystal ball. It's the first one I've ever had. My anger settles into a calm storm and the way becomes clear. The orb makes a satisfying crunch as I swing it into his cheek. I hit him hard, harder than I think. His light goes out as he falls, red blossoms blooming on skin, accompanying his last breath. Selena rises from the bed, shock set on her face. I see that she has a new rose tattoo like mine.

Did Rob know it wasn't me?

It doesn't matter now.

"For someone who sees the future," I say, "you see very little." I close the gap between us and hit her with the orb as well. She falls unconscious on the bed.

I dress her in my clothes and with some disgust put on hers

which I pick up from off the floor. I carry her to the balcony and look at the rock garden below. It's only two floors down, but the rocks are sharp. I laugh because I never wanted the stupid garden anyway. What a fitting way for her end.

A bit of a heave and she's over; the rocks below fulfill their task. Almost. I think I see her move. I aim the crystal ball at her head, and throw.

I take a deep breath and walk downstairs to call the police.

"Poor troubled Bianca," I say through streams of tears. "I saw there would be bad things in her future, but she wouldn't get help."

They comfort me, the needy sycophants Serena called her friends.

The man who smells of coconut and summer puts an arm around me. He says, "Oh, Serena. How terrible."

"What will be, will be," I say, shedding just the right amount of tears.

A Spell

Hocus-Pocus

don't lose focus!

Pinch of sugar and fat.

Eye of spider,

hair of lioness,

cunning of a rat.

Touch of royalty,

three sharp blades.

#spell to make a cat

Be Gone

"There's something in our room," I say.

"Come," it says. It pulls at me.

"Leave us be," I say. The pressure eases – slightly.

Next to me in bed your snoring deepens. You never hear it, John. I wonder when you became so closed off, so distant? I sit up and look outside. My reflection is distorted in the glass and my features seem to merge. Is this really me? I feel like I look – haunted.

I lie back down, pull the blankets close, snuggle against your warm back. Your skin turns to gooseflesh at my touch. You shift, pull away, cry out. I wrap my arms around you and say that it's all okay. You whimper, but this time you do not resist. Your warmth fills me.

I hold you tight, and I drift away.

I dream of many things. Holidays together, our wedding, our plans to have children. Why didn't we have children, John? I can't remember. Odd things fill my thoughts. Scruffy, before he died. Your mother at a funeral. Our old school friends, all in black. You looking very sad.

Why are you sad, John?

I wake, and you are not in the bed. You must be getting a drink, or something.

"Come," it says, again.

I turn away.

<hr>

I wake in agony. I'm being pulled apart. "Be gone," an unfamiliar voice commands.

You stand next to a priest – crying! You look bad, John.

But when did you find God, John? Why is God in our home? I see a new addition to our room, a crucifix upon the wall. These changes make me angry.

"Get out," I scream. A wind swirls cold, your skin prickles again. Lights flicker on and off. The priest's resolve weakens, and he clutches a rosary tighter. I pick up my jewellery box from the dresser and throw it as hard as I can. It hits the priest on the chin. He drops the bible and flees.

"John," I yell, but you flee too.

I cry and go away, back into my dreams.

<hr>

Hit by a truck, right outside. I remember now. There was an accident. But who was hurt? Scruffy runs onto the road and we follow. He barks and barks, a screech of brakes, then...

Then everything shifts. I see you running, nervous, looking over your shoulder. You are hammering boards on the bedroom door. What are you doing? Why are you like this?

<hr>

I awake in our room again. The bed is empty, the crucifix tilted on the wall. The Bible lays open on the floor, the priest's rosary and a splash of his blood on its pages. My spilled jewellery box spews trinkets dulled with dust on the carpet.

I try to find you, but I feel so, so tired.

"Come," it calls, again. I turn away once more.

<hr>

I wake. Something is different in the dark. The bedroom is empty, abandoned. Dust is thick everywhere. Why am I still here?

I have to find you, John. I tear through the house, calling, searching.

Crucifixes are everywhere. An army of crucifix soldiers step down the stairs in place of our artwork.

I find you in the kitchen, hunched over your coffee. Broken. Tears stream down your face.

"Leave me alone!" you say.

I reach to you, but you pull away.

Behind me a dog barks. It's Scruffy.

"GO!" you yell. "Leave me in peace," you plead.

Scruffy comes to sit between us. Finally, I understand.

I'm dead, I say. I draw close and whisper in your ear. "I stayed because you said we'd always be together."

Your eyes go wide like dark pools. A whimper squeaks from your throat.

I squeeze you, tight, tight as I can.

Scruffy barks and barks.

I take your last breath, then I finally go.

We can be… together.

<hr>

Vapour thin you rise, alone.

"Come," it says, but you pay no heed.

"Where have you gone?" you ask the empty house.

PUSH

I know the weekday morning drill by heart: make you breakfast, pack a lunch, grab a coffee, open the laptop – pray that it starts. You stay away, get dressed, get ready for school. Today the laptop does start, and I scan the wanted ads, mark the possibilities. I'm still making notes as you leave to catch the bus. You slam the door, leaving a late but cheery farewell in your wake.

"Have a good day," I yell after the whirlwind that is you.

Returning to my routine, I revise cover letters, tweak the resume, send off two applications and prepare to send a dozen more. I make another coffee. As I return the milk to the fridge, I notice the unpaid bills stuck on by magnets. More bills than ever before. The notices billow as I shut the door, waving, reminding me they are there.

Then the front door opens and sheepish and guilty you mumble you've missed the bus. Everything goes on hold. In a blink I'm shucking off my slippers and slipping into a familiar resentment about things not going as they should. I curse your father for dying, for leaving me in this mess, and I curse you too, even though I know it's not your fault. The unpaid bills wave at me again as I grab the car keys, telling me to get a job. To do better. To be better. Maybe I'll get the job from yesterday's interview. But who can ever tell?

Onwards I push. Push. I push you out the door. "Be better," I say to you, regretting saying it and justifying saying it, confused about feeling I have to say it.

The road is busy; too busy. I pull out to overtake the bus. I don't listen to what you say. Maybe I don't want to hear. I'm angry – at you, at me, at it all. Maybe, if I'd been that little less upset, I would have heard the panic when you called out—

The metal twists and shrieks and shattered glass rains in. A pent-up hiss, an airbag releases against my chest. Yours doesn't deploy. It all becomes a haze. The scent of burnt hair and flesh; a copper taste coats my tongue. You—

I try to look, but something blocks my way. Are we next to the bus, or in it? My vision adjusts and I see a stranger's eyes in your place, broken eyes, un-seeing eyes.

And then it's all too much…

and I'm somewhere else.

We're in the hospital; it's the day of your birth. Your brown eyes stare, wide and trusting. Tears stream down my cheeks. I'm so happy you are here. Your father is here, too.

Then your eyes become a stranger's eyes, and everything melds and melts; folded metal, shattered glass. My heart races me awake to searing pain. Monitors beep and white walls surround me. A nurse holds my hand.

"Where…?"

"There was an accident," she says. "A bus… A semi-trailer…"

I feel the impact, remember seeing your eyes—

She gently squeezes my hand. "I'm sorry about your son…"

An injection into my IV and I begin to float. Words dissolve into nothingness as I turn away. My phone rings on the cabinet next to me. I reach to turn it off but press the speaker on instead.

"Congratulations!" It's the voice from yesterday's interview. "We'd like to offer you the job."

I push the off button. I don't know if I need a job anymore.

I push, and push, and push it all away.

LINEN

Hammering in Dad's workshop sets the beat.
We dance the washing line, Mum pegs.
Birdsong joins laughter as we peekaboo through
billowing, crisp linen.
Sun-drenched and joyous, with me forever.

WOODEN SPOON

The slap reverberates around the room. My five-year-old brother sounds an alarm. In seconds, Mum storms in, apron around waist, flour-covered hands clutching a wooden spoon. I'm only seven and small. She's a giant.

"So," she says. 'What happened?'

Her stare says *I'm at fault. Again.*

"Sh-sh-she took my car!" my brother says.

"Give it to me." Mum holds out her hand.

She gives the car to Matteo. Whack! The sharp rap of wood across my knuckles stings. Matteo stops crying, as though that was his reward. Mum returns to her baking, leaving hints of vanilla, a trail of flour and her disapproval behind.

Matteo holds the car like a trophy while I cradle my throbbing knuckles. Funny how he's stopped crying now. Funny how he has what he wanted even though it was mine. Mum always says, *Girls don't play with cars.* Even though I'd been given the car as a gift, in this house a car is for a boy.

My reddened knuckles now match the welt on my wrist where Matteo had twisted my arm. I should have cried when he grabbed me. I should have made some noise. It wouldn't matter now if I showed Mum what he'd done, showed her the red, finger-shaped marks.

But that wasn't what upset me. Something else hurt. Matteo was not firstborn, but he was the one that wore the weight of the lineage. He was the one that mattered. I wore the shame of being a girl.

I remember as if it's happening today, almost twenty years later.

The yelling from one of the bedrooms snaps me back. I wait instead of rushing in, stay seated and keep typing on my laptop at the dining table. The volume on the TV increases, presumably to block out the children's cries.

"Remember when we used to go away on holiday and I'd fish off the pier with your father?" Mum says from the couch in front of the TV. "You and Matteo, playing in the dunes on the beach. You were such good children."

She comes for one four-hour visit each week. Four hours gets longer each visit. I inwardly cringe. Family holidays were a nightmare. I remember my teenage brother shoving seaweed in my mouth, throwing sand in my eyes. I tried not to go swimming because he would hold my head under water. At fourteen he was taller and stronger than me.

My son comes out, tears flowing. Ben is five. He holds a car in one hand, a doll in the other. His left cheek is bright red. He points towards his older sister. I stand up, hands on hips. Annie is in the doorway, looking like she's done something wrong.

"So," I say. "What happened?" My voice is, in that second, my mother's.

On the couch my mother has turned, her glare – the same glare she's practiced for years – burns into Annie. "Come here, Benny." History unfolds. "Did Annie hurt you? Naughty Annie. Come sit on Grandma's knee and I'll give you a cuddle."

"I have it under control thanks, Mum." My mouth is full of sand.

Ben comes and climbs onto my lap. I hug him, encourage him to tell me what happened, find a tissue in my pocket to wipe his eyes. He says, between solid and loud sobs, that Annie took his toys and hit him, hard.

Annie inches backwards, shame across her face.

"Send her to her room!" yells Mum.

The twenty-year-old memory, the wooden spoon. My knuckles smart again. But I'm not seven anymore.

"You've had your turn being a parent," I say, but I'm shaking.

I call Annie over. A few more questions reveal Ben snatched the car from Annie and fell over when he did and that's how he got the mark.

"It's not Annie's fault you hurt yourself, Ben." I hold my hand out and Ben gives me the car.

I put my arm around Annie and draw her in. "Ben says he took this from you." Annie is relieved. She hugs me back. "So, what were you playing in there anyway?" I ask.

Mum turns her attention back to the TV. Crisis over, she's lost interest. I settle the kids to some quiet play and come back to my work. The television drones in the background. Mum snores lightly on the couch.

Gentle laughter comes from the bedroom now. Ben's found my lipstick and has red lips and rosy red cheeks. Annie has built a parking garage out of Lego. My heart fills with love for my children. David comes in from the garage and slips an arm around my waist. "We're pretty lucky, you know," he says.

I draw him in a closer. He's right. We are. We watch the children play for a few moments longer.

"They are growing up in a different world, thank goodness," he says, nuzzling my hair. I savour the warmth.

As I'm collecting Mum's things to take her home, my phone sounds. It's a message from Matteo. He wants to know how Mum is. "Just checking in," he says. But he doesn't really care. He never calls her at the home. This is the fourth message I've had in two months. I delete the message immediately because I think he's just waiting for his inheritance. He's still waiting for Mum to give him something, even as a grown-up.

"Say goodbye to Grandma," I yell out as I close the front door. The only voice that comes back is my husband's. I feel a pang of sadness, but, then again, Mum made her choices long ago.

As the door clicks closed, Mum yells from the car, "What's taking so long? I must be back by four. It's movie time, you know."

It's only three thirty and the home is ten minutes away. It's the same discussion, every time, no matter when we leave. "You'll be back in plenty of time, Mum." The car door slams shut and I wonder how many more visits there'll be. As I drive, the litany of complaints spills forth about how I manage my family. I tune it out, like I did the loud TV, and think about what I'll do when I get back. Maybe we can all go to the park. Maybe we'll play dress-up. Or maybe I could play some Lego with my daughter.

Maybe we could build a garage for our cars.

One thing's for certain: there won't be an episode with a wooden spoon.

Waves

roll in…
recede…

We are the waves, we are the tides,
we are endless and eternal.
In the expanse of our oceans,
we experience much,
we abstain from world affairs
and do not get involved.
Try not to get involved…

roll in…
recede…

In moonlight's ghostly spill,
You sit on the pier.
savouring the quiet moments
before the breaking of dawn.
You are our friend – the keeper of the sands,
collecting beach-combed garbage,
each day, taken from the water's edge.

roll in…
recede…

Footsteps swift and light
grace the wooden planks behind You.
So light the steps,
You do not notice Her approach.
The old and sturdy pier murmurs not;
if only it could.
She
is so silent – which is not Her usual way.

roll in…
recede…

A hatred exudes from Her
a toxin to the pure, morning air.
We recoil.
Her intent is
Is…

roll in…

We splash the pylons; spray our brine.
But our waves only reach so high,
our collective cries unheard
resound with a gentle splash.
We cannot warn You.
Our agitation wasted,
our reach falling short.
We draw back
and back.

recede…
recede…

You turn to face Her,
Your calm is gone.
Replaced by something
questioning and painful.
She greets You with Her
true, hateful, self:
the one she never shows.
A sound reverberates
through the pylons of the pier
and then
You fall.
Fall. Into us.
Your lifeblood spills, salty and metallic,
Until there is no more.

roll in…
recede…

Something falls in after You.
Is it the implement that hurt You?

roll in…
recede…

You float, Your warmth soon stolen
by our cold caress.

You are garbage adrift,
like that You once collected.
But who will collect You?
We mourn.
Duty-bound, we accept You, our friend,
into our ocean heart.

roll in…
recede…

On the pier, She greets the morning sun –
instead of You.
Light shines upon Her, but
darkness radiates from within Her –
like a big black sun.
Her last act of revenge
is to kick Your garbage from the pier
and cast Her wedding band as well.
Then She goes,
leaving it to us.
We swallow down the sharp edges
of Her bitterness
and Her deed.

roll in…

We hold You, wrap You
nurse You in Your endless slumber,
cradled in our ebb and flow.
She is long gone

when the sun reaches mid-sky
and crowds fill the sand…
and we return You
to the beach You walked so many times.
And we ensure, before sending You ashore,
that within your clothes You hold Her ring,
and the thing that caused Your doom—

roll in…
recede…

DIMINISHED

We stand at the edge holding hands.
Summer scents mingle with salty air;
water tickles our toes.
Is this how it ends?
Our bodies diminished;
our memories distorted by time.

What's Left Behind

Ayla's scarf flaps in the wind and a flutter of pink printed butterflies take flight. Pale skin blends against white sand, pink shorts and tee make a bright beacon on the shore. She breathes in the ocean scent, salt bitter on her tongue. Waves roll in fast and frothy to break at her Mary Janes. Seagulls shriek in a blue sky, a dog barks, someone whistles in reply.

Sitting on her haunches, Ayla's shorts scrape the sand. She uses the driftwood to poke the seaweed, looking for a treasure.

"No getting wet!" Grandma yells from a bench seat near the dunes, shawl wrapped tight against autumn air. Hands rest on her cane, eyes ever watchful.

Ayla waves and turns away. "Don't get wet, blah blah blah," she says to the receding water. Grandma was fun, once. Now all she does is worry and nag.

Through the tangled kelp, something shimmers. It's a shell.

"Ayla, Ayla!"

The tide rolls in, licks her shoes. Coolness tugs at her toes. She looks around – Grandma stands alert. Ayla groans and resettles on drier sand, but it's too late. Grandma is coming over. She wishes that sometimes they could all stop fussing. Doctors, nurses… she is sick of it all.

The shell catches the sunlight. Like a pearl, it's iridescent, but with pinks and blues and purples. It spirals like a pointed turban, no bigger than a ten-cent piece, a fitting home for a tiny crab. She shakes it.

"Whatcha got, Ayla?" Grandma takes a while to sit down.

"Look," Ayla says, holding it out.

"It's beautiful, just like you." Grandma turns the shell in Ayla's small palm. Her hair brushes Ayla's fingers, hair the same silver as the outside of the shell.

"Did you know that a shell's colours are formed by what the mollusc eats?" Grandma says.

Ayla considers this new information. *What if eating fairy floss made you pink?* Would they let her just eat fairy floss? She's just about to ask if she can experiment, but Grandma keeps talking.

"You know, shells are parts of creatures, and if one's empty, like this one, the mollusc inside has died."

Dying. Adults usually don't mention dying. They speak about how "advanced" things are, but always stop when she's around. She only hears because she eavesdrops. Grandma says this is the last beach visit before hospital. Ayla doesn't want to go to hospital.

Her feet are cold now, wet.

"Will I leave something beautiful behind when I die?"

Grandma hugs a bit too tightly. "Ayla, all that remains of us in time are what we leave behind: our actions and the memories we make. People remember us through many things: a photo, an action, an item. These are the things that remind us."

Ayla gives Grandma the shell. "I want you to remember me like this, Grandma."

"As a beautiful shell? What a lovely memory." Grandma's voice trembles.

Ayla looks at Grandma's wrinkled palm. The shell has dried, its colour faded. "Can you remember me as sparkly and pink?"

FRAGMENTS

Marie sat at the park bench, gaze on the playground, mind on other things. Jack was late with the fortnightly payment again, and he wouldn't take the kids for the weekend. They needed new school shoes, but she didn't have money. She needed to go to work, but couldn't afford a sitter. The pipe under the sink was busted, and who was going to fix that? But these were all worries for another time. Right now, she was spending time with her children.

Tinkles of laughter drifted up from somewhere far away. Her two angels.

"Lovely day today."

The man's voice was familiar, but she couldn't place it. The uncertainness and interruption unsettled her.

She clenched her jaw. "Can I help you?"

He was six-foot-tall, smartly dressed. Maybe in his 40s. But he wore mirrored glasses.

"Don't trust someone if I can't see their eyes," she said. "Eyes tell you a lot about a person. My Jack's eyes, for example—"

"I know," the man said, laying a hand on her arm. "But you're safe with me."

"How can I be safe with someone I don't know?" Her laugh was light, dismissive. She shook him off and walked to the play equipment.

"Where are they? They were here, playing..." Her voice tapered off.

"Come on, Marie. It's getting cool, let's—"

"How do you know my name?" She felt unsettled now, things were not as they seemed. She drew back when she caught sight of her reflection in the mirrored glasses. She touched her face, felt the deepened lines. She was old; much older than she thought. More wrinkles, more worry lines. When had her hair become so grey? A feeling of futility clutched at her chest.

"I know you. We are… family. Come on. Let's look inside the building over there."

Marie looked where he pointed. The place gave her the chills.

"Are you a police officer?" Marie asked. "They look like the glasses that motorbike police wear on TV." She looked at the building again. "I don't want to go over there. Where are my children?"

The man's shoulders slumped. He'd been through this before.

"Did you take them?"

"Maybe Jack has taken them to get ice-cream," the man said.

Marie whipped around, fast. He wasn't prepared. "Jack wouldn't do shit for my kids. Who are you?" and with a quick swipe, she knocked the glasses from his face.

"You're him! The one who keeps following me!" she said. "I'd know those eyes anywhere."

He signalled for a nurse. His mum was crying and yelling and telling him to leave. Each time he'd come to visit, he'd had to find a new disguise – a way to mask his eyes. Was it the glasses, though, or something that he'd said?

Maybe next time he could do something different, and they could just hang out, like they used to. He'd have to speak to the nurse again and see what she suggested.

"Bye, Mum," he said, as the nurse took her inside.

Pieces

Deadlines close around me like vultures at a stocktake sale. It doesn't matter to anyone else I have work to do. I mean, working from home, it's not a real job, right?

"Mum, can we have curry for dinner?" says one.

Sure, why don't you cook it?

"Can you pick my order up from the computer store?" says another.

I mean, you have a car, so…?

"Is there any yoghurt?"

Can't you open the friggin' fridge door?!

I want to say these things, but they won't come out. I swallow them down, down to somewhere else – another existence. I'd created this mess myself because I've always done what they asked. But how to change it? I am the matriarch; I do my job well. But it comes with such a personal cost. They aren't babies anymore, my children. They tower over me, can drive and even have jobs, but somehow it's always *Mum, Mum, Mum*. I'm truly sick of it and I don't know how much longer I can keep going. But keep going I will, as I always do.

I pack up my work, know it will still be here after dinner and the day, and go to do the tasks. Smiling, even. My resentment presses down, in the practised way I'm used to, so I barely know it's there.

And with this thought, the first piece of me floats away.

It's an odd feeling – a gentle brush against my neck, a whisper, soothing, soft like a summer breeze. *Let it go*, it seems to say. I pay it no attention. I have things to do.

The next pieces I lose are at the supermarket. When I reach into the meat section to grab a steak – *screw a curry!* – I leave more of me behind. At first I think my skin has stuck to something cold. But my hand is intact.

I toss the steak in the trolley and move on. When I reach into the freezer to get ice-cream – *do they even deserve ice-cream?* – the feeling happens again. Is it freezer burn? But once again my hand looks fine.

I stand between the ice-cream aisle and the shelves of toilet paper staring at my hands, holding them out in front, weighing the empty air. They look the same, but the left one is heavier than the right. Is the left one a bit denser, too? No. I shake my head. Laugh a bit as well. *Why would I think that?* I stare at them for a while longer, so long that a shop assistant asks me if I needed a "hand". I return a frosty "no, thank you," and head to the checkout. People snigger in my wake and my face turns red. I let out a deep sigh as I turn the corner.

A piece of something else leaves on my breath. I panic a bit, wanting to reach the safety of home. Of the familiar and the solid. The routine and life I know. The more I try to grasp inside myself for something secure, the more anxious I become.

I load the groceries from the trolley onto the conveyor belt, not listening to what the cashier says after "hello". As I reach for the peas, I see my right index finger fall off. But when I blink, my hand is still intact.

"Did you see that, or am I going mad?" I ask, jokingly.

The cashier's look says madness. She moves a bit away.

When I reach into my bag to get my wallet, I can't pick it up. I swap hands to pay, then have to load the bags into my trolley left-handed.

"Umm, are you okay?" asks the cashier.

I want to scream, *No, I'm not! Can't you see something is wrong?* But I smile and say, "Everything's fine, thank you."

Another piece drifts off my shoulder. My bag slips and I only just catch it. I must look ridiculous. I push the trolley with some effort. I don't feel very substantial at all. After what feels like an age, I finish loading the shopping in the car.

I go to the computer store, as was requested. I use my left hand to pay and ask the storeperson to carry the small box for me. I say my hand is sprained and I am struggling to lift things. He looks at me funny, like he knows it's a lie, although he helps me take the box to the car anyway.

After my jobs I drive home. Straight home. *Without yoghurt.* It's getting stronger now, this feeling of losing myself. More pieces fly away.

All my angry and confused thoughts coalesce and assail me. *I should have let them do things themselves. Why do I say yes when I want to say no? What is wrong with me?* I can't find the answers and only end up annoying myself.

Now, as I look in the rear-view mirror, more wisps of me float away – from my hair, my shoulders, everywhere.

I stop checking behind and focus on the road ahead. The Peninsula Hot Springs turn is ahead and for a moment I consider going there instead. I tell myself I'm far too busy to go – now or anytime in the near future really – and maybe one day I will, when I don't have so much to do at home. We moved here as a lifestyle choice, but for me it doesn't matter our address – my lifestyle is always the same.

As I turn into my driveway, my left hand sinks into the wheel. I can't even see my right hand anymore. As I pump the brake, my foot goes through the floor. I stop the car, somehow, mere centimetres from the house.

I'll be honest. I sit in the car for a while in tears. But the longer I cry, the more of me comes out. When I try to open the car door, I can't grasp the handle, not with my left hand or my right. In exasperation I nudge the door with my shoulder and partially go through it.

I try to blast the horn, but before I can I am sinking, sinking through my seat. Everything slips away, and as I disappear completely, I wonder if I have ceased to exist.

———◆——◆———

When I come to, I am standing on the footpath, outside my home. I am not the same me as I was before. I am a collection of all the pieces I've given away. In my car sits the other part of me, the part who always says yes. I watch her as she opens the door and gets the shopping out, smiling, even humming, unaware she's lost anything at all.

A hand slips into mine. It is made up of someone else's lost pieces.

"Come on," they say. "What do you want to do now?"

My own lost pieces arrange themselves into a smile. "You know, no one's asked me that in a very long time."

They give my hand a small squeeze. "We don't have to do anything, if you don't want to," they say.

And with those words, I realise I am finally free.

Invisible

They're invisible,
elusive,
always flying free.
They're in the air
or of the earth
and sometimes of the sea.
But these pieces – when I catch them –
all belong to me.

THE DREAMS THAT SHAPE US

Threads of golden light teased the horizon and hushed the katydids' yearning calls. The forest's nocturne gave way to cicada chorus and the song of birds.

Miirai seemed to stretch with the sunlight, her multicoloured trunk reflecting the pinks, golds, and oranges of the morning; even Liido's grey trunk wore a gleam of gold. Their silver leaves shimmied with daylight-dipped edges.

But Liido wasn't feeling so bright. Miirai's notions were becoming increasingly irrational. Excitement seeped through her bark, like sap, as she talked about her dreams. "Crow says if I want, I can change. I have to wish, very hard."

"Nonsense. We start as seeds and grow as tris. We can't just change like that. Our roots tie us to earth. We are grounded, cannot move. A tri does not walk."

Miirai's brightness dimmed and her enthusiasm dampened.

In the silence Liido's ire grew. "And wish? Crow is a trickster and a fool. He flies high, sees nothing. You cannot move, Miirai. Tris stand firm and tall." The Elders had cautioned a wariness of Crow for as long as he could remember, and he'd given Miirai the same warning many times. "Crow fills your thoughts with unachievable dreams."

"Dreams are what shape us," Miirai said.

Liido knew this to be true but was surprised Miirai had said it. She was certainly growing up. He felt a moment of pride before her next words snatched that away.

"What do I have keeping me here?"

Her rebuke wounded, as was its intent. Whipbirds' calls rent the air and insects stilled, silenced by the growing tension. Less than a foot separated Liido and Miirai aboveground, but they were a tangle of roots below. As they stood together on the hill, a breeze lifted and meshed their leaves together. Miirai fought to pull hers away.

"We have each other," he said. The words felt hollow, as though they rattled without meaning in his aging trunk. Their conversations always ended like this lately. It wasn't easy being separate from the other tris, and he ached. He had tried to shield Miirai from the pain of detachment, but he could see now that she felt it acutely. Still, he was older. It was his responsibility, and his alone, to protect and guide her.

"We have many things that enrich our lives, Miraii. The sun warms us, wakes the animals and the birds. The moon's soft glow bathes us and we drink its peace. Night's veil brings the nocturnes, and the songs of the forest fill us with tales of friendship and love. The wind whispers through our leaves, and the rain cleanses and provides. Creatures live in our leaves. The natter of the plants and grasses is a melody. What could be better than standing here, tall, proud, and on top of the world?"

Her temper was hot. "I knew you wouldn't understand. You never understand. You had the others. I didn't. I don't like this life. I yearn to have contact, to see other sights, to be free—"

"Free? What is this if not free?"

"You don't listen. You have the soul of a tri, Liido. Not like me. I have the soul of a *wild horse*. A brumby!"

Her heat flared at his roots again, then disappeared. And like that, his sense of her was gone. "If you keep doing that, all your buds will drop off and you won't flower," he said in a huff. "You may have the longing of wild horses, but you are still a tri."

She'd been right, of course, about being alone. They had been for almost all of Miirai's twenty rings. She wasn't a sapling anymore, but she wasn't an adult either. Liido had no clue how to deal with her now. He wondered how the Elders managed their difficult youth. He had no one he could ask.

Even after all this time, he missed touching the roots of others. His memory held the feeling of their dying embrace – the last pulses sent out, looking for nourishment, only to be denied. If Liido were ever cut down, the scars of separation would show in his rings not as fine lines as the rest of his years did, but as jagged cuts etched deep, lined with sap, like large, gaping wounds.

Liido imagined Miirai's first-year lines were similar. Maybe her scars were deeper than his. It was times like this he wished that the family had taken him and Miirai as well, cleared them away from their land with the others. Then he would have never known this grief, or had to make these choices.

He reached out through the soil, hoping again to find another, to seek counsel from the Elders. But the only conversation to be had was one-sided, receiving nothing more than a burble of sounds from plants with shallow roots. Grass could never convey a complex message to the Elders, nor receive one. And the flowers: the self-indulgent, sex-starved decorations that were only interested in insects and pollination.

Underneath the groundcover, the earth began to thrum. The grass stopped its song and Liido pulled back to his trunk. The vibrations moved stronger and closer, the grass keening a familiar tune. Someone from the farmhouse was mowing. Liido preferred the sheep nibbling nearby grass, but lately they were in a different field. This made his loss even more acute, as he thought of the family down the hill, the herd of sheep with their own kind. He retreated into his trunk as far as possible as bits of shorn grass flew onto and around him. His bark had been nicked by the machine once, and it had stung like a million bees.

———◆——◆———

Miirai opened a small channel so water could flow from her roots. She felt Liido's deep frustration, but also his deep love. For some reason, this made her even more irate. If he loved her, why didn't he understand? She was a caged spirit that needed to be free, and he was holding her down.

Distantly aware, a knot throbbed in her trunk. The midday sun was taking moisture from her leaves. Bark would peel and flake, and leaves would fall from her branches, if she didn't drink. And then Liido would have something else to criticise.

He was probably still moping around, sulking because she'd made it clear she wanted to go. He was happy here on the hill; she wasn't. But she wasn't asking him to leave. And why would he want her to stay if she didn't want to be here? She was angry and annoyed with him, too. Just because his roots reached deeper and he had more rings in his trunk, it didn't mean he knew everything.

The water moved through her, and she concentrated on this instead. Feelings of the earth filled her. The grass had been cut earlier, and its lament imitated the sound of the cutting machines, mirroring her sadness. She opened channels wider, feeling for the comfort in the pain, and found something else. She'd almost missed it by being closed off. Her branches quivered with joy, and she opened the channels even wider, questing through her roots away from Liido and down the hill.

A herd of brumbies ran across the rocky outcrop in the distance. Her pulse quickened. Lots of separate hoofbeats, some lighter than others; there were young ones in the pack. Their movements played up her trunk to her leaves, filling her.

She tried moving with them, imagined using her branches like legs. Tan, black and white moved through the distant tris, hooves clambering and thudding on hard earth. She could see herself running with them — a flash of silver, limbs pummelling the ground, wind feathering a leafy mane, her trunk damp with a sheen of effort, heartbeat thrumming and water sluicing through her veins.

"I see you've found your inner peace," said Crow.

Miirai jumped, jittering her branches.

Crow hung on tight. "Did I startle you?"

Her rosy bark took on a heightened glow. Crow always made her feel special. "I was having the most wonderful time," she said. "Is this inner peace, when you are finding your desire?"

"Some say yes. If you were still connected to the tris, they would have taught you about inner peace and about forest magic."

"Forest magic? Is that how my spirit flies free?" Liido had never spoken of magic.

As if reading her thoughts, Crow replied, "Liido may not know about magic. He was young, too, at the Clearing. The magic is passed down from Elders. An ancient wisdom shared through linking with others of your kind."

"How is it you know these things?"

"I share the same world, under the same sky. The rules for tris are the same for the plants and animals, even the humans. There are things available to all of us that are lost when we are separated from our communities. When you do this – when you think of yourself elsewhere – it helps you find your own connection. It can help you discover forest magic."

"Am I doing it right? I disconnect and dream when I'm in my leaves. Is that magic? But why is it that the earth connects me, grounds me, when I'm questing with my roots?"

"You must practice, Miirai."

But she had been practising. Crow seemed to know what he was talking about, though. She'd just have to keep trying. An emotion that wasn't hers stirred on the fringes of her roots. Oh no, she'd opened herself to—

"Ah, Crow," said Liido. "Filling Miirai's thoughts with fantasy? Disconnection? Forest magic?"

"Liido!" said Miirai. "Stop!"

"I've looked after you all these years. I have never lied. Crow tells half-truths to tempt you. The magic is for the Elders. The rest, we have shared."

"But have you shared, Liido? I don't think so," said Crow.

Miirai felt Liido's anger seeping towards her and Crow. And for the first time in her life, Miirai doubted Liido's concern was for her. "I need some time to be alone," Miirai told Crow.

Liido's voice fell away as she slipped into the stillness of her leaves. Her dreams returned to running with the brumbies, tails flicking and sweat shimmering as they capered, while flocks of lorikeets fluttered and whirled in a clear blue sky.

◆——◆——◆

Liido had not expected Miirai to depart so suddenly. Crow sat in her branches, laughing and picking at her leaves.

A flock of lorikeets squawked as they flew noisily toward them, but upon seeing Crow they veered away, shrieking their message to others to avoid the tri in which Crow sat.

"I was protecting her," Liido said, almost to himself. "I didn't share some things, like how to quest, because I am not an Elder. It fell to me to keep her safe."

"Keeping her safe or keeping you safe?" said Crow.

Liido would not admit this could be true. "Why do you taunt her so, Crow? What have you to gain?"

"Liido, Liido. I do so for my amusement. Besides, she might really be able to run. How do you know, in your limited view on this isolated hill, that she can't?"

At first he'd felt guilty for spying on her while she was dreaming, but now he was glad he had. Now her dream made sense. She really believed she could change; it wasn't just a fantasy. Legs of bare silver branches and a mane of leaves. Is this what Miirai wanted? To have legs? To run? Liido wished he'd paid more attention to Crow's earlier visits and conversations. He wondered what else Crow had told her, but he dared not ask.

He withdrew from Miirai completely, cutting off Crow. He made a half-hearted attempt to quest with his roots, but once again he fell short. Rather than face Crow with his failure, he looked to his own leaves to try to understand what Miirai looked for in herself. The space he found deep within felt hollow, unwelcome. He could almost feel all of his leaves, separately, as if he were two parts. His isolation from his brethren amplified, this place echoing his deep loss. And thirst, such thirst! No hope was here, only sadness, maybe madness. It just felt wrong. Was this where Miirai went inside herself to escape? There was no magic here.

When he came back to himself, it was dark. Stars blinked through languid clouds in an indigo sky while a quarter moon stood watch. The evening nocturne had resumed, the katydids and other creatures calling for their lovers. It was a different world. Crow had been replaced by a still and silent barn owl. The only movement was its head, ever so slightly, as it tracked something in the field.

Lights flickered like large stars in the farmhouse below. Branches snapped afar under the weight of night creatures large and small. The evening air was chilled, clouds increasing a distant grey.

Owl, focused on his target, leapt from the branch, breaking through the calm.

"I want to be a brumby," Miirai said.

Nothing had alerted Liido of her return, and his response was automatic and untempered. "How can you be a brumby? You have branches and leaves. Foolish ideas, fuelled by foolish Crow." He felt the now-familiar rage scald and was immediately sorry.

"You kept secrets, Liido! Crow has told me."

"I've shared everything I know about being a tri, shown you what to do, how to live. I've done as best I can, Miirai."

"No, you haven't. You were part of a family. The other tris talked to you, nurtured and held you nestled in their lineage. Could you give me this? Could you bring the dead ones back? Could you?"

Realisation dawned on Liido. She was born of the pain. When the trees were cleared from the hill to only leave one, Miirai was such a tiny sapling she hadn't been seen and was spared. They looked and felt as one, but were two. This is why Miirai had never been able to find herself – she had always felt like part of Liido.

When he was with the other tris, he was separate but part of the community at the same time. Miirai had never felt that. He'd never thought to teach her how it worked.

Her voice was soft and full of despair. "There has only ever been you."

"And Crow," he said, finally understanding. Miraii longed for the things he'd been trying to shield her from. His loss of a family was hers as well.

Now they stood together and separate, hurt on both sides creating a gulf between them. For the first time since the Clearing, Liido felt alone.

⁍———⬤——⬤———⁌

Liido's remorse washed over her, but it was too late. She withdrew again, leaving him to find his own solace.

The sky turned steel, and rain sprinkled branches and leaves. Below, grass sang in gentle supplication. Miirai enjoyed the rain, too, light or heavy. It made her feel alive. She imagined her bark was skin, the drops washing her rather than feeding her, sloughing away the old and rejuvenating the new. Crow said washing was a human thing, but Miirai felt it was true for tris. She pictured her limbs as human arms, her leaves forming hands that cupped the falling water.

Then, the smallest jolt, and an unexpected one at that: one of her branches responded. A small swaying and swish of leaves, but a definite twist upward, toward the rain.

The sun's rays broke through a patch of cloud, warming her trunk, making her branches more limber. Excitement shot through her.

Miirai focused on a single limb, sending everything she had to the one branch. Her trunk groaned and retracted, fuelled by channelled water and stored energy. The branch twisted further skyward before becoming rigid and still.

She'd moved! But something felt wrong. She opened all her channels at once, seeking more nutrients, connecting to her roots, but some were not responding.

She could see her dream now, taste it. Crow had been right, after all. She pushed harder.

Leaves and small twigs fell from her branches as she reached. Great strips of bark peeled away, and where they should have revealed more of Miirai's colourful trunk, the tones were dim shades of grey. Sap leaked from smooth knots, as though her very lifeblood was escaping. Her leaves sagged, and many fell to the ground.

"I can do it," she said.

———◆———◆———

Liido stalked her edges, lending her support, sending her nutrients. Miirai's pulse was weak. Small branches and leaves were strewn on the grass below in haphazard piles. Her trunk was dull silver and smooth, a ghost newborn of her former self. Her limbs, without foliage and smaller twigs, looked long and sleek, as if ready for movement. Newly formed buds burst through the remaining leaves, and Liido wondered if she'd have the strength to bloom.

What had she done? It was much too soon to flower. He did something he'd never done before. He sent his roots questing along hers, exploring her secret spaces, invading her forbidden realms. But he couldn't find her anywhere.

Surely it wasn't possible. Could Crow have spoken some

truth? Could she change?

In the distance, at the far edges of his roots, he could feel a tingling, the whisper of another tri. Of all the times for this to happen! After all this time! But Miirai's heartbeat fluttered and weakened, her pulse slowing even further. With an almost audible groan, he pulled back his energy and sent it to her instead. He would search for the tris again later. Miirai needed him now.

As the clouds darkened and lightning twisted overhead, Liido imagined himself cradling Miirai in his branches, keeping her safe from herself.

***

Liido stirred from a light slumber. Early morning shadows hung like weighted blankets on his branches. Miirai's trunk was even duller than before. Sunrise was dreary when it wasn't reflected by her colourful bark. The grey seemed to absorb all the light and not give anything back.

He felt for Miirai, coming back with no sense of her other than her pulse. It was stronger now, but it felt somehow wrong. Altered.

"Miirai," he called. "Miirai!"

"She can't hear you," Crow replied, sitting in his branches.

Liido resented feeling Crow's talons on his branch. He wondered why Crow was sitting there instead of with Miirai.

"She's getting ready," said Crow.

Something *was* happening. Liido felt cold, even though the sun was out. He shuddered, his leaves shaking without a breeze. Miirai was drawing all the heat, soaking it up like parched earth did the rain. Steam misted around her.

"What's happening?" asked Liido.

"Watch," said Crow.

On Miirai's dull silver trunk, near the ground, a deep-orange mark was forming, growing, expanding upwards.

"Mirai!" Liido called. "Where are you?"

With a sickening grind that reached him through the earth, Miirai's trunk split open along the orange line. Amber oozed from the gaping wound.

What was she doing? The heat was still building in her trunk, radiating out like a midday summer sun. It was as if Miirai was soaking it all up, storing it, using it to—

"Miirai! No!"

In a surge of energy, Liido was pushed back, both their trunks groaning with the unseen strain. Crow's talons dug deep as he maintained his perch.

Golden light shot up and into her branches. As it touched her leaves, every bud burst into a red flower. And with the light, her spirit leapt into the morning sky.

Liido leaned forward. "No!" Her trunk felt empty. She had gone.

"Well, look at that," said Crow as he flew away. "I didn't think she could."

✦

So many moons pass that Liido stops counting. He misses her every day. From a distance, the two old tris atop the hill look to have grown together. One hunches over the other as though holding it, keeping it safe. It's impossible to see where one's branches start and the other's stop.

Liido keeps Miirai's trunk alive, supports her husk for her return. Their bark is dry and rough, their trunks colourless and dull, their leaves sallow and scarce. The family at the bottom of the hill wonders occasionally if they should cut them down. Crow visits with the weight of her loss on his wings, saying he is sorry for what he has done. Liido does not answer.

<hr>

Liido doesn't notice the nocturne anymore. He doesn't hear any other tris. His slumber is long, and he spends more time asleep than awake. Today he feels not so bad, but he's always tired, and some days he doesn't wake up. He hears the grass singing its welcoming song to the dew. The flowers chatter, light and frivolous. The house lights shine below, humans waking before dawn for daily duties.

Brumbies' hoofbeats echo in the distance. A stray brumby neighs as if calling to another. There's a strange warmth next to his side, and as he tries to leave the last sands of slumber behind, he feels something he's not felt since the days before the Clearing.

Nuzzling his bark is a silver brumby.

"Miirai?" he asks drowsily.

The brumby whinnies, as if in answer, and gallops down the hill. The sun rises to an empty paddock.

Liido draws deep through his roots and slowly comes to. There's no sign a brumby was here; he can see no crumpled grass. Liido sets about feeding Miirai, tending to her needs before he tends to his own.

There's an itch on his side where the dream brumby was. He imagines she nipped him, to let him know she was there, but then he laughs at how old and foolish he's become.

The grass copies the sound of a horse galloping down a hill and Liido drifts back to sleep, dreaming of a life in the company of tris.

Mirri, You're Not Real

Mirri's skin is vellum soft, she's delicate, demure.

Her words glimmer, incandescent pearls. She lives in my dreams.

Mirri begs to have a heartbeat, I refuse.

She cries neon tears.

Acknowledgements

Writing is a solitary pursuit. When I write horror, I dig deep, find what hurts or moves me then build it into stories to be shared. The aloneness in the process, however, is only in the creation. Once the story is written, it's the writing family and the production team that lift it up. Thank you to the Horror Crits group and Chris for all your feedback and to Clare for yours as well, and to Noel and Ché for editing and production. A special shoutout to Lynette, for working with ridiculous deadlines to produce a most magical cover. To my husband – as always – thank you for supporting what I do, even if you don't like reading stories that are dark. Last but not least, thank you to the readers who read my stories and buy my books.

About the Author

Louise Zedda-Sampson is an award-nominated Melbourne-based author, editor and researcher, who writes in many genres. Her short stories are in the genres of literary, speculative and horror fiction, while her non-fiction writing covers topics ranging from hauntings to history to sport. Louise's fiction and edited works have been shortlisted, longlisted and received honourable mentions in various competitions and awards, and in 2022 Louise was awarded the Rocky Wood Memorial non-fiction scholarship by the Horror Writers Association (HWA). Louise's debut non-fiction book, *Bowl the Maidens Over: Our First Women Cricketers*, was released in 2021.

Also by this Author

Bowl the Maidens Over: Our First Women Cricketers
The Cocktail Connoisseur's Message Cards
The Cocktail Connoisseur's Recipe Book

Visit Louise's website for a full list of awards and publications
www.LouiseZeddasampson.com.au

About the Stories

"Close to You", Writers Victoria Flash Fiction, online 2021

"The 504", *Haunted*, Specul8 Publishing, 2021

"The Forgotten Sea", *Antipodean Issue 250*, 2019

"Dark in Here", *Supernatural Drabbles of Dread*, Macabre Ladies Publishing, 2021

"Scrunch", Writers Victoria Flash Fiction, online, 2021

"End of the Line", *Dark Recesses Press Webzine*, 2022

"A Stranger With My Face", *Nightmare Fuel Magazine*, 2022

"Measure", Writers Victoria Flash Fiction Contest, 2020

"Broken", *Guilty Pleasures and Other Dark Delights*, Things in the Well, 2019

"Sparkle", Writers Victoria Flash Fiction, online, 2022

"A Warm Embrace", original to this collection

"He Said There'd Be Chicks", *Nightmare Fuel Magazine*, 2023

"Confinement", *Infected 2: Tales to Read Alone*, Things in the Well, 2020

"Drift", Writers Victoria Flash Fiction, online, 2020

"The Beating of Her Heart", *Midnight Echo 16*, AHWA, 2021

"A Shadow in This Red Rock", *From the Waste Land*, PS Publishing, 2022

"Droplets", *Extreme Drabbles of Dread*, Macabre Ladies Publishing, 2020

"Mistakes", original to this collection

"A Spell", Writers Victoria Flash Fiction, online, 2020

"Be Gone", *Nightmare Fuel Magazine*, 2022

"Push", *Pendulum Papers,* 2023

"Linen", Writers Victoria Flash Fiction, online, 2020

"Wooden Spoon", *Page & Spine*, 2021

"Waves", original to this collection

"Diminished", Writers Victoria Flash Fiction, online, 2020

"What's Left Behind", *Somers Paper Nautilus Issue 73*, 2018

"Fragments", *Pendulum Papers,* 2021

"Pieces", original to this collection

"Invisible", original to this collection

"The Dreams That Shape Us", *Brink Issue #4*, 2022

"Mirri, You're Not Real", Writers Victoria Flash Fiction, online, 2022